AN AMISH ALPHABET

INGRID HESS

Delightful illustrations and simple, respectful prose—a lovely book!

—Steven M. Nolt, author of *A History of the Amish*

Ingrid Hess has captured the essence of Amish life.

—Jane Hoober Peifer, Mennonite pastor and children's author

The stunning images are a gateway for young children to enter the world of Amish people.

—Ervin Beck, researcher of Mennonite and Amish folklore

A delightful book that combines accurate information, tasteful design, and a sampling of Bible verses that Amish people learn by heart and treasure all their lives.

—Ann Hostetler, professor of English, Goshen College

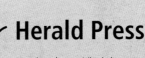

Herald Press

Harrisonburg, Virginia
Waterloo, Ontario

Library of Congress Cataloging-in-Publication Data

Hess, Ingrid.
   An Amish alphabet / Ingrid Hess.
      p. cm.
   ISBN 978-0-8361-9645-0 (alk. paper)
   1. Amish--Dictionaries—Juvenile literature. I. Title.
   BX8129.A6H47 2012
   289.7'3--dc23

                                   2012014851

AN AMISH ALPHABET

Copyright © 2012 by Herald Press, Harrisonburg, Virginia 22802
       Released simultaneously in Canada by Herald Press,
       Waterloo, Ontario N2L 6H7. All rights reserved.
Library of Congress Control Number: 2012014851
International Standard Book Number: 978-0-8361-9645-0
Printed in United States of America
Illustrations, along with cover and interior design, by Ingrid Hess.
Photography by Pavel Romaniko

Scripture text is quoted, with permission, from the New Revised Standard
Version, © 1989, Division of Christian Education of the National Council
of Churches of Christ in the United States of America.

To order or request information, please call 1-800-245-7894 in the U.S.
or 1-800-631-6535 in Canada. Or visit www.heraldpress.com.

16 15 14 13 12   10 9 8 7 6 5 4 3 2 1

 **is for Amish.**

The Amish are a group of Christians known for their simple, old-fashioned way of living. Most of them live in the country. They don't have televisions, and they don't drive cars, wear the latest fashions, or join the army. They want to serve God and live in peace together. Amish people try to obey the teachings of Jesus in the Bible.

Therefore come out from them, and be separate from them, says the Lord, and touch nothing unclean; then I will welcome you.
2 Corinthians 6:17

**is for barn raising.**

Barn raising is an old tradition that is still practiced by the Amish. If a farmer needs a new barn, Amish neighbors gather to build one in a single day. Everyone has a job. Some saw wood and others hammer nails. The little boys fetch parts and tools. The women and girls make a lot of food.

C is for church.

The Old Order Amish do not have church buildings. Instead, they meet in homes every other Sunday. A special wagon pulled by a horse brings benches and song books to the home before the church service begins. The family places the benches in the house. Men and women sit separately. Services usually last about three hours.

The God who made the world and everything in it, he who is Lord of heaven and earth, does not live in shrines made by human hands.
Acts 17:24

D is for dress.

The Amish dress very simply. Women wear long, plain dresses without stripes or designs. Straight pins hold their Sunday dresses together. Women also put on prayer coverings or black bonnets. Men wear plain shirts and pants that are held up with suspenders rather than belts. Their coats and hats are black in the winter but they wear straw hats in the summer. The Amish do not wear jewelry or wristwatches. Because of their simple, plain clothes the Amish are often called the "plain people."

Do not be conformed to this world, but be transformed by the renewing of your minds, so that you may discern what is the will of God—what is good and acceptable and perfect.

Romans 12:2

F is for farming.

Most Amish live in rural areas. Amish farmers grow corn, hay, wheat, and alfalfa. Much of what they grow is used to feed their animals. Rather than using tractors, the Amish rely on horse-drawn equipment with steel wheels. Vegetable gardens provide food for the family and produce for roadside markets.

G is for German.

Many Amish use three different languages: Pennsylvania Dutch, German, and English. Pennsylvania Dutch, a type of German, is spoken with other Amish people during everyday life. Children learn English in school so that they can talk with non-Amish people, whom they call "the English." In school, German is also used. Bibles used by the Amish are in the German language.

# H is for horse and buggy.

Instead of cars, most Amish use horses and buggies to go places. The Amish believe that horses and buggies help them stay close together as they build families and try to be faithful to God as a church. A horse can travel more than twenty miles a day, averaging ten miles an hour. They can't go far in a horse and buggy, so the Amish usually stay close to home.

I is for idol.

The Amish do not want their pictures taken. Why? They don't want to be self-centered. Pictures highlight individual people, not the community. Amish believe that posing for photographs is showing off. The Amish also believe that making pictures of people is like making an idol to worship. God is the only one who should be worshiped.

You shall not make for yourself an idol, whether in the form of anything that is in heaven above, or that is on the earth beneath, or that is in the water under the earth.
Exodus 20:4

J is for Jakob.

The Amish church was started in Switzerland in 1693 by a man named Jakob Ammann. He and his followers belonged to a larger group of people who believed that baptism was only for adults who chose to be baptized, rather than for children. These people were called Anabaptists. Jakob Ammann's group was stricter in its way of living than some other Anabaptist groups, such as Hutterites, Mennonites, and certain Brethren.

K is for kitchen.

An Amish kitchen is the center of the home. Preparing, preserving, cooking, and eating food are important parts of Amish family life. Amish women are known for their delicious cooking. Restaurants that serve Amish food and cookbooks that feature Amish recipes are quite popular.

Waterloo Region

**Elkhart County &
LaGrange County**

**Holmes County
Lancaster County**

L is for location.

The Amish live in five hundred close communities throughout North America. In the United States the largest Amish communities are in Holmes County in Ohio, Lancaster County in Pennsylvania, and Elkhart and LaGrange counties in Indiana. In Canada, the Amish live in southern Ontario, many in the Milverton, Aylmer, and St. Jacobs areas. Because Amish families have an average of seven children, the Amish population is growing. The number of Amish people in America has doubled since 1990.

M is for music.

The music in an Amish worship service is different from most church music. The Amish sing slowly, in unison, and without instruments. Some Amish songs last more than twenty minutes! Amish song books have the words of the songs but no musical notes. Melodies pass from generation to generation.

P is for prayer.

Both at worship services and at home, the Amish usually pray in silence, or they read written prayers or recite the Lord's Prayer. As a sign of respect for God, Amish women wear prayor coverings on their heads. Women and girls do not cut their hair.

Any woman who prays or prophesies with her head unveiled disgraces her head—it is one and the same thing as having her head shaved.
1 Corinthians 11:5

Q is for quilt.

Amish quilts are known for their beauty and excellent quality. Like the Amish community, the whole quilt is more important than any of the individual pieces. Quilting brings the women of the community together. Their carefully made bedspreads may be used in their homes or sold in order to help someone in need.

R is for Rumspringa.

At age sixteen, before they are baptized as young adults, Amish young people enter a time called *Rumspringa* (German for "running around"). Because they are not yet baptized, the church rules do not apply to them. During Rumspringa, Amish youth decide whether or not they want to receive baptism and join the Amish community. During this time they are also allowed to date.

S is for social security.

Unless they work for businesses outside their community, the Amish usually do not have to pay social security taxes, which help take care of people in their old age. The Amish provide their own social services. The elderly, for example, are always cared for as respected members of the community. The Amish do pay other kinds of taxes, such as federal, state, and provincial income taxes, as well as school and sales taxes.

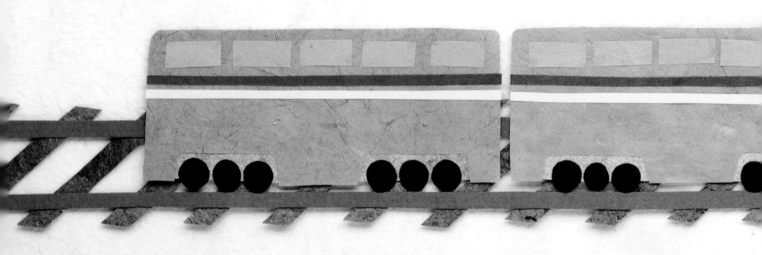

T is for trains.

When Amish people need to travel a long distance, using horses and buggies isn't practical. Instead, they travel by taxi vans, buses, and trains. They do not travel by plane.

U is for unshaven.

It is easy to tell if an Amish man is married—just look at his chin! Before they are married Amish men shave. After they are married they let their beards grow. Amish men do not grow mustaches because they have been a sign of military service.

V is for vegetables.

The Amish plant large gardens and raise much of the food they eat. The Amish also sell their crops in produce auctions across the country. During the summer months food is frozen, canned, and dried to preserve it for use during the winter.

God said, "See, I have given you every plant yielding seed that is upon the face of all the earth, and every tree with seed in its fruit; you shall have them for food."
Genesis 1:29

W is for woodworking.

Farming is not the only work that Amish people do. In the United States alone there are more than twelve thousand small Amish businesses, such as machine shops, construction firms, and food services. The Amish are also known for their high-quality woodworking. They make cabinets, furniture, and children's toys, including the popular marble roller.

X is for xxxxxxx.

Crazy quilts, made by Amish women, contain random shapes of fabric pieced together then connected with decorative stitches. One often-used stitch is called the cross-stitch. Each beautiful crazy quilt is one of a kind.

Y is for Yoder.

Because the Amish community has remained close for many generations, the number of family names is somewhat limited. Yoder is a common family name. Other common names are Stoltzfus, Miller, Fisher, Troyer, and Bontrager. The most common first names for Amish men and boys are John, Amos, Samuel, Daniel, and David. The most common first names for Amish women and girls are Mary, Rebecca, Sarah, Katie, and Annie.

Yoder's Tomatoes

lies, the Amish rise at the crack of dawn.
They wake up so early and work hard, so
bedtime falls earlier for them than it does
for many people.

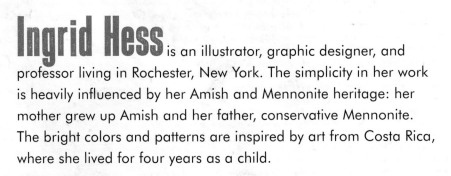

Ingrid Hess is an illustrator, graphic designer, and professor living in Rochester, New York. The simplicity in her work is heavily influenced by her Amish and Mennonite heritage: her mother grew up Amish and her father, conservative Mennonite. The bright colors and patterns are inspired by art from Costa Rica, where she lived for four years as a child.

Ingrid holds an MFA in graphic design from Indiana University with an emphasis in the book arts and has worked in the publishing industry since 1996. Her dual passions of design and illustration work well together and help her tell stories through pictures. Her research focuses on economic justice as a way to bring peace to the world.

Ingrid is author and illustrator of Herald Press titles *Sleep in Peace* (2008 Rodda Book Award winner) and *Walk in Peace*. She also wrote *Think Fair Trade First* in which she seeks to empower children to understand that they can make a difference in the world.